8/03

SO-AJM-359

Put Beginning Readers on the Right Track with
ALL ABOARD READING™

The All Aboard Reading series is especially designed for beginning readers. Written by noted authors and illustrated in full color, these are books that children really want to read—books to excite their imagination, expand their interests, make them laugh, and support their feelings. With fiction and nonfiction stories that are high interest and curriculum-related, All Aboard Reading books offer something for every young reader. And with four different reading levels, the All Aboard Reading series lets you choose which books are most appropriate for your children and their growing abilities.

Picture Readers
Picture Readers have super-simple texts, with many nouns appearing as rebus pictures. At the end of each book are 24 flash cards—on one side is a rebus picture; on the other side is the written-out word.

Station Stop 1
Station Stop 1 books are best for children who have just begun to read. Simple words and big type make these early reading experiences more comfortable. Picture clues help children to figure out the words on the page. Lots of repetition throughout the text helps children to predict the next word or phrase—an essential step in developing word recognition.

Station Stop 2
Station Stop 2 books are written specifically for children who are reading with help. Short sentences make it easier for early readers to understand what they are reading. Simple plots and simple dialogue help children with reading comprehension.

Station Stop 3
Station Stop 3 books are perfect for children who are reading alone. With longer text and harder words, these books appeal to children who have mastered basic reading skills. More complex stories captivate children who are ready for more challenging books.

In addition to All Aboard Reading books, look for All Aboard Math Readers™ (fiction stories that teach math concepts children are learning in school) and All Aboard Science Readers™ (nonfiction books that explore the most fascinating science topics in age-appropriate language).

All Aboard for happy reading!

For J, N, & K, of course — R.A.H.

For my daughter Paris and
my friend Ronnie — B.O.

Text copyright © 1996 by Ronnie Ann Herman. Illustrations copyright © 1996 by Betina Ogden.
All rights reserved. Published by Grosset & Dunlap, a division of Penguin Putnam Books for
Young Readers, 345 Hudson Street, New York, NY 10014. ALL ABOARD READING and
GROSSET & DUNLAP are trademarks of Penguin Putnam Inc. Published simultaneously in Canada.
Printed in the U.S.A

Library of Congress Cataloging-in-Publication Data

Herman, Ronnie Ann.
    Pal the pony / by Ronnie Ann Herman ; illustrated by Betina Ogden.
        p.   cm. — (All aboard reading)
    Summary: Pal the pony is too little to participate in the rodeo but becomes the star of the
ranch in a different way.
    1. Ponies—Juvenile fiction. [1. Ponies—Fiction.   2. Ranch life—Fiction.   3. Rodeos—
Fiction.   4. Size—Fiction.]   I. Ogden, Betina, ill.   II. Title.   III. Series.
PZ10.3.H465Pal   1996
[E]—dc20   95-30265
                                                                                          CIP
ISBN 0-448-41257-8   2002 Printing   AC

PAL THE PONY

By R. A. Herman
Illustrated by Betina Ogden

Grosset & Dunlap • New York

Pal is a little pony.

He lives on the Star Ranch.

Today is a big day.

It is rodeo time.

All the cowboys and horses
get ready.

Blaze runs all around
the ranch.

She wants to be
the fastest horse
at the rodeo.

Pal tries to run fast, too.

But his legs are too short.

Samson pulls and pulls.

He will pull the big wagon

for the hay ride.

Pal tries to pull, too.

But he is not very strong.

Kicker kicks and bucks.

He is the best bucking bronco.

Pal tries to kick
and buck, too.

Oops! Down he goes.

Poor Pal.
He is too little
for the rodeo.

So he just nibbles some grass
and swishes his tail.

Nibble, nibble.

Swish, swish.

A little girl sees Pal.
"What a cute pony," she says.
"Do you want to ride him?"
asks a cowboy.

"Yes!" says the girl.
So—trot, trot, trot—
off they go.

They go past the barn,

past the pond,

and—trot, trot, trot—
back again.

The little girl hugs Pal.
She gives him an apple.

"You are my pal,"
she says.

Now all the children
want a ride.

Pal does not run
or pull or kick.
Even the littlest child
can ride Pal.

Pal is the littlest pony
on the Star Ranch.
But Pal is the biggest star
of all!

1.3